CHANNING O'BANNING
AND THE TURQUOISE TRAIL

ILLUSTRATED BY
TAMMIE LYON

BY
ANGELA SPADY

Tommy NELSON®

A Division of Thomas Nelson Publishers

NASHVILLE   DALLAS   MEXICO CITY   RIO DE JANEIRO

Channing O'Banning and the Turquoise Trail

© 2015 by Santa Cruz Press, LLC

Published in Nashville, Tennessee, by Tommy Nelson. Tommy Nelson is an imprint of Thomas Nelson. Thomas Nelson is a registered trademark of HarperCollins Christian Publishing, Inc.

Tommy Nelson titles may be purchased in bulk for educational, business, fund-raising, or sales promotional use. For information, please e-mail SpecialMarkets@ThomasNelson.com.

ISBN-13: 978-0-7180-3236-4

Library of Congress has cataloged the copyright

Printed in the United States

15 16 17 18 19 RRD 6 5 4 3 2 1

Mfr: RRD / Crawfordsville, Indiana / April 2015 / PO #

*To Steve . . . for drawing
warm memories onto my heart.*

Table of Contents

1

Dig In!

"There it is! There it is!" said my best friend, Maddy. She used a paintbrush to sweep away the dirt and get a closer look.

"Are you *sure* we're supposed to use a paintbrush for this?" I asked. "This is weird, Maddy. Very weird."

I wondered if my best friend knew what she was doing. After all, *I'm* the expert when it comes to using art stuff.

"Oh, but it's *not* weird to keep a pencil stuck in that ponytail of yours?" Maddy asked. "I wouldn't talk about weird if I were you, Channing O'Banning!"

Maddy did have a point. But I liked to be ready to draw at all times. Having a pencil in my ponytail made perfect sense to me.

"As for my paintbrush, this is how they do it on *Quest for Bones*. I'm positive," Maddy continued.

"She's right," Cooper interrupted. "They use all kinds of different brushes to sweep away dirt. Once, they uncovered a fossil that was actually a dinosaur egg."

Cooper always explained every single thing he'd seen on *Quest for Bones*. He told us whether we asked about it or not.

"Hmmm . . ." Cooper said, pushing his glasses back up on his nose, "I wonder if cavemen ate dinosaur eggs for breakfast? That would be one big omelet!"

Maddy and I stared at Cooper like he was an alien. Sometimes his brain was on another planet. *Who cares if cavemen ate omelets?*

We got down on our hands and knees and looked closer at the rocks. We'd been digging in the same exact spot for a whole week. On days when it was too cold to go outside, we stayed in at recess and planned our next move.

The whole thing started when Cooper dared me to race him to the end of the playground. Of course, I would have easily beaten him by a mile if I hadn't tripped over a dumb rock. I even tore a hole in my zebra high-top sneaker. It was *totally* embarrassing. Not only did I trip on a rock and wreck my favorite shoes, but I let a boy beat me in an easy race. That was just plain wrong.

But the rock that tripped me didn't look like any normal rock. It was gray in some spots and white in other places. Part of it was sharp and part of it was smooth.

So Maddy and Cooper decided to start digging and digging and digging. Did I mention there was digging? Because there was—*every single day*. Cooper and Maddy were sure there was something amazing buried under the Greenville Elementary playground, but I didn't really care. I just wanted my friends to get more interesting hobbies, *ASAP*!

We'd even been studying about rocks in Mr. Doring's science class. Boring Doring gave each one a fancy long name that I could barely pronounce. *Why can't rocks have non-weird, easy-to-remember names?*

"Got any other ideas of what it might be, Maddy?" Cooper asked anxiously. He had rocks on the brain.

"I'm not sure, Coop," Maddy answered and continued to brush away dirt. "I wonder if it's some sort of fossil."

"Really?" Cooper squealed. "That would be so cool. Maybe there are arrowheads under there too! Dig harder, Maddy! Dig harder!"

"Move out of the way, Cooper, and let me get a better look," I insisted.

"Don't be so bossy, Channing O'Banning. If it weren't for me daring you to a race, or should I say *beating* you in a race, we wouldn't have made this discovery in the first place."

"Don't remind me," I mumbled. "I wish I'd never agreed to your crazy challenge. I could have saved myself a shoe! Come on, let's go do something else."

Anything has to be better than this. Even playing on the monkey bars. My palms get sweaty and I usually end up falling off before I'm even halfway across. But even *that* is better than digging in the same boring spot for all eternity.

"Hey, Chan," Maddy suddenly asked, "will you do a sketch of the rock for us? You never know, we might need it later."

Yes! Finally, something I like to do. Scratch that— something I love to do!

I looked closer at the dig site and pulled my Gray Elephant colored pencil from my ponytail. Nana bought it for me when I was into drawing African animals, so that's why I named it Gray Elephant. It was times like this that I was glad to have a pencil close by. Plus, it looked cool in my ponytail. I drew a picture of our dig site in my sketchbook. Drawing was much more interesting than playing around in the dirt, anyway. Before long, I was finished with my sketch.

"Want me to help brush away the dirt, Mad?" I asked. *The sooner we get to the bottom of this, the sooner we can do something else at recess.*

"Sure, Chan, but try not to damage anything. This might end up in a museum or something."

"A museum? That would be awesome!" Cooper screamed at the top of his lungs.

"Shh . . . not so loud!" Maddy whispered. "We don't want the whole school knowing about our discovery yet! Anyway, we have to stop digging and go to social studies class. Bummer."

"Oh, why does that goofy bell ring just when we're getting to the good part?" Cooper whined. "I wish we could wait and have social studies class tomorrow."

I didn't mind going to our next class. Social studies was one of my favorite subjects, besides art, of course. Mr. Reese always made class fun and sometimes even a little crazy. When we studied about ancient Egypt, he came to class dressed up like a mummy (Cooper almost fainted). When we learned about China, Mr. Reese gave everyone a fortune cookie and even showed us how to use chopsticks. No matter how hard I tried, I could *not* get my fingers to hold them the correct way. I almost poked Maddy's eye out just trying to pick up a wad of paper.

This week we were supposed to study Native Americans. It sounded totally boring.

"Don't be such a grouch. Learning about Native Americans might be fun," Cooper said.

"Not to me. You guys are such nerds. I wonder which Indians he'll talk about today. They all seem the same to me—*bor-ing!*"

"Not really, Chan," Cooper said as we walked into class. "They're all really different. And they're called Native Americans—*not* Indians. Don't you remember what Mr. Reese said yesterday?"

I didn't have a clue, but luckily, I could tell Maddy didn't either, which made me feel a teensy bit better. Sometimes my BFF and I get busted for talking in class and not paying attention. Come to think of it, yesterday was one of those days.

"Native Americans lived here long before we did," Cooper pointed out. "The only reason they were called Indians is because Columbus thought he was in India when he landed here."

Now I was really confused, but I didn't dare admit it to Cooper. I didn't see why we had to study this sort of stuff.

"Columbus traveled to India?" Maddy asked. "Wow, I had no idea."

"You still don't, silly," Cooper laughed. "Columbus was in North America but *thought* he was in India. He didn't realize he'd blown off course and was way over in America."

Cooper traced the distance from America to India on a map. "Crazy, huh?" he asked.

"Yeah, crazy!" I blurted out without thinking. "I guess you could say that Columbus really lost it!"

Everyone laughed at my joke. Even Mr. Reese giggled a little.

After checking attendance, our teacher had a surprise for everyone. Mr. Reese brought out a small cardboard box from his supply closet and set it on his desk. Maybe we were getting new pencils? Or maybe he'd brought candy for all of us? *Maybe* he had gummy turtles for the entire class? Then he'd be my favorite teacher forever!

But Mr. Reese reached inside the box and pulled out three things: a tiny blue rock, a pot with two holes in the top, and a plastic dinosaur. *What is he up to this time?*

Weird. Very weird.

2

The Mystery Box

"Class, today you're going to learn some interesting facts about Native Americans and the Wild West!" Mr. Reese said.

It did sound sort of fun, especially the Wild

West part. I looked closer at the things from the box. I'd never seen a blue rock before. And it was such an amazing shade of blue—sort of like the ocean.

Why couldn't a rock like that be out on the playground? Then I might be interested!

I grabbed a blue pencil from my backpack and quickly drew the rock in my sketchbook. I needed a good name for that pencil but hadn't thought of one yet.

Surely Mr. Reese would tell us more about this rock before the bell rang. I pulled the gray pencil from my ponytail and replaced it with the blue one, just in case I needed to use it again.

"Remember, kids, there are more than two hundred tribes that live in North America. Each has its own unique way of life," Mr. Reese said, pointing to the large world map.

"Wow," Cooper whispered. "I thought that only the Cherokee and Apache lived in America. I used to watch western movies about them with my grandpa. They were awesome!"

"I guess there are more tribes than you thought," I whispered back. "But if Mr. Reese makes us memorize every single one, I don't know what I'll do. I'm afraid I'd get a giant F for flunk-o-rama."

"He won't be my favorite teacher anymore, that's for sure!" said Cooper.

"Told ya. Studying about this stuff is going to be a total brain drain," I whispered back, rolling my eyes. "One of these days you people will listen to me!"

The Native Americans seemed boring, but I still wanted to know more about that blue rock.

Suddenly I noticed Mr. Reese had stopped talking and was staring straight at us. It was like he had teacher radar and could read our minds.

Yikes.

"Cooper, Maddy, and Channing, would you three like to stand in front of the class and tell us more about Native Americans? You seem to enjoy talking to one another."

I got a lump in my throat and quickly looked down at my neon pink high-tops. Maddy buried her head under her social studies book. Cooper froze like a statue.

"As I was saying, there are many tribes in North America. For example, the Zuni live in Arizona and New Mexico," said Mr. Reese. "They create beautiful works of art, including pottery and colorful tribal jewelry. Channing, would you like to make a poster on Native American art?"

Huh? Why on earth would he ask me that?

"Oh, uh . . . I guess I could, Mr. Reese," I stuttered. "Okay . . ."

Why don't Coop and Maddy have to do extra work?

"Another group we'll be studying about is the Apache. They rode horses, hunted buffalo, and lived in amazing tepees," Mr. Reese pointed out.

That's when Cooper freaked out a little. "Oooh! I wish I was an Apache!" Cooper squealed at the top of his lungs.

Everyone in the entire class heard him. His face turned as red as the poison ivy rash he had last year.

"Cooper, would you like to do a report on the Apache?" asked Mr. Reese. "You seem quite excited about the subject."

Yes! At least he got busted for talking too!

"Cooper is such a big nerd," Maddy whispered. "The next thing we know he'll be building a tepee in his backyard."

But before we knew it, Mr. Reese had given every person in class a ginormous project. This was going to take forever. He must have studied in college how to torture fourth grade kids.

"Are you *sure* the Navajo still exist, Mr. Reese?" Maddy asked, trying to weasel out of her assignment.

Maddy liked talking about social studies, but she wasn't a fan of doing big projects.

"I'm sure, Madison. Once you've completed your report, I bet you'll be an expert."

"Mr. Reese is definitely *not* my favorite teacher anymore," Cooper griped. "We'll be working on these projects until we're twenty!"

The clock on the wall said 9:45 a.m. We had only a few minutes left.

"Mr. Reese, are you going to tell us more about those things on your desk?" I asked. "The bell is about to ring."

Cooper reached over and poked me with his pencil. "Why are you asking that, Chan? We don't need any more homework! Geez!"

Sometimes Cooper could be so bossy. I tried my best to ignore him.

"Thank you for reminding me, Channing. All of these items are found in the states of New Mexico, Texas, and Nevada," Mr. Reese said, smiling.

He picked up the pretty blue rock and gave it to Cooper to pass around. "Class, this is turquoise, a valuable stone found in the West. Often people must dig extensively to find these rocks. But once they find them, they're polished into beautiful rocks like this one."

I had to have a closer look.

"Hurry, Coop! Hand it over! Let me have it!" I insisted.

"Now who's acting like a nerd?" Cooper asked, finally giving me the rock. The turquoise felt cold in my hands and had little gray lines running through it, sort of like veins. I suddenly knew exactly what to name my blue pencil: Totally Turquoise!

Mr. Reese then picked up the clay pot with two holes in the top. It looked strange, since it had two holes to pour from instead of one. *Weird. Very weird.*

"Hold it gently, everyone. This is a wedding vase made by the Zuni tribe in New Mexico. Before a marriage, the bride drinks out of one side, and the groom drinks out of the other."

The vase was brownish orange with all sorts of special markings on it.

"Don't drop it, Chan," Cooper joked. "You can be a real klutz, you know!"

Why Cooper thought he was funny, I had no idea. I looked closer at the drawings on the sides of the vase. I was sure they meant something, but I didn't have a clue. If only we could make this kind of stuff in art class.

Mr. Reese held up the last object on his desk.

"This is a model of a tyrannosaurus rex. These dinosaurs have been found in the West as well."

"Wouldn't it be awesome to be a paleontologist?" Cooper exclaimed as he turned it over in his hands.

Maddy and I both look confused.

"You know, one of those people who looks for dinosaur bones," Cooper explained.

Actually, that didn't sound awesome at all. Having to spend all day, every day, 24-7 digging around in the dirt and looking at rocks and bones? I could think of a zillion other ways to spend my time that would be more interesting. Like watching paint dry.

But if I did find a dinosaur in the dirt, I bet I would make a ton of money. And a ton of money would mean a ton of colored pencils. Plus drawing dinosaurs was actually pretty fun.

Maybe being a paleontologist wouldn't be the worst thing ever, after all.

3

Boring Doring

Science was the last class of the day, which was a total bummer to me. It was my worst subject, so I always went home in a bad mood. Why couldn't every day end with art class? Now *that* would be *perfecto*!

But instead, I had to sit and listen to Boring Doring. He could talk for hours and hours about rocks. Blah, blah, blah. I even fell asleep in his class last week. No one noticed until I fell out of my chair with a loud flop. I'd drooled all over the desk and my hair stuck to one side of my head. *It was totally embarrassing.* The whole class, even me, couldn't help but laugh. I hope I never fall asleep in class again.

But if Boring Doring talks about blue rocks or even dinosaurs, then I *know* I'll pay attention!

"Class, get into your seats, please. We have some very exciting things to do!"

Mr. Boring waved his arms like it was some kind of emergency. "All of you will find out today that school really rocks!"

"Science teachers should never try to sound cool. *Ever*," Maddy whispered.

"You can say that again!" whispered Cooper.

Boring Doring's square glasses sat crooked on his nose, and his white hair went every which way. He looked like one of those crazy scientists about to bring a monster to life. He talked forever about the differences between sedimentary, igneous, and metamorphic rocks.

"I didn't realize there were so many different kinds," said Cooper. "I just want to get them out of our way on the playground."

Cooper was right. Rocks were the only things keeping us away from our big discovery. However, I did like the turquoise rock that Mr. Reese showed us in social studies class. But Mr. Boring never talked about rocks like that. He only talked about brown, dirty, boring rocks.

"Let's review a little. Who can tell me what a person who studies rocks is called?"

"Crazy!" yelled someone from the back. Jeremy

Jackson thought he was the class comedian. He was also the one who bombed every test. Mr. Boring didn't think he was very funny.

"Is it a geologist?" I asked, crossing my fingers.

Cooper acted shocked that I knew the answer. Just because I like pencils in my ponytail doesn't mean that I'm a dingbat.

"Bravo, Channing O'Banning, you are correct!" said Mr. Boring.

Maybe our teacher wasn't as bad as I'd thought.

He went on to show us pictures of different kinds of landforms that were made up of rocks. "Sometimes rain, wind, and gravity can cause the landforms to change. This is called *erosion*. That's how valleys, mountains, and canyons are formed. Sometimes erosion helps geologists make big discoveries."

"Well, I know the name for guys who look for dinosaur bones!" Cooper said, trying to be a showoff. "They're called *pa-lun-tol-o-gists*!"

"That's correct, Cooper," said Mr. Boring. "But it's pronounced *pay-lee-un-tol-o-gists*."

"Why does Cooper think that only guys can look for dinosaurs?" I whispered to Maddy. "Who does he think he is, anyway?"

"Oh, Cooper's just trying to be a know-it-all,"

Maddy said loudly, hoping that Cooper heard her. "He thinks he's the class brainiac."

Actually, he *was* the class brainiac. Maybe Maddy was a tiny bit jealous.

"Madison Martinez, since you like talking so much, why don't you tell me again the three types of rocks in the earth?" Boring Doring asked.

Uh-oh.

I could tell that he didn't think Maddy knew the answer. What if she'd been daydreaming the whole time? This could be bad. This could be *really, really* bad.

"Sedimentary, igneous, and metamorphic," Maddy said proudly.

I couldn't believe it! Our teacher looked as surprised as the rest of us.

"That's correct, Madison!"

Cooper and I looked at Maddy like she was from Mars.

"Who are you and what did you do with my friend Maddy?" joked Cooper.

"Yeah, tell her to come back to planet earth," I added.

"Oh, knock it off, you two," Maddy whispered. "I guess I've dug around in those rocks so much that they're kind of . . . well . . . *interesting.*"

"I can't believe it. I *cannot* believe it. Maddy Martinez is turning into a rockologist!" said Cooper.

"A geologist," I corrected him. I bounced a paper wad off his head while no one was looking.

Boring Doring went on and on about the layers of the earth and pointed to a giant poster on the wall.

But. Then. It. Happened. I was starting to get sleepy . . . *really, really sleepy.*

I could barely keep my eyes open.

"Tomorrow we're going to study about some very interesting minerals," said our teacher.

My eyelids felt like they weighed ten zillion pounds. I couldn't fight it any longer. I was becoming a sleeping science zombie.

"Everyone should get ready for tomorrow," he said. "You'll be learning all about diamonds, rubies, and turquoise."

Turquoise?

My eyes flew open quickly. Had Boring Doring talked to Mr. Reese? Did he have a turquoise rock too?

Suddenly the bell rang for class to end. And for the first time in my life, I wished that science class could last a little longer.

4

Computer Crash

After school, I had to refocus because I had a job to do: beat my sister, Katie, home from school. I call her the Snoop. It suits her perfectly. If I was going to figure out if I was digging up a dinosaur, not to mention about to score a goldmine of colored pencils, then I had to do it before the computer hog got home. If she beat me to it, I'd have to wait until I was forty-five to log on.

I ran as fast as I could down Darcy Street.

Oh, please, please let me get there first!

By the time I got to the door, I could barely breathe. My legs felt like limp noodles. I needed water . . . and gummy turtles, of course. But Katie was already sitting at Mom's computer. She even had her feet propped up on the desk.

Nooooo!

"Do you have to be on the computer, Katie?" I whined.

She gave me her usual eye roll. Sometimes I wished her eyes would get stuck like that.

"As a matter of fact, I do need to be on the computer. My friend Bethany told me about an awesome song to download. Then I'm going to get online and chat with Mia for a while."

I wanted to scream.

"Katie, all of that stuff can wait," I insisted. "I need to get on the computer now! It's an emergency!"

"Yeah, sure, Chan. Sure it is," Katie said, not believing a single word. "Guess you'll have to stand in line and wait a while, shrimp."

Ugh! But when Katie tried to turn on the

computer, it wouldn't even come on. She tried again and still had no luck.

Ha. Ha. Ha!

"Looks like you don't even know how to use a computer!" I said. "Poor Katie. Maybe Mom can buy you a plastic one at the toy store."

"Oh, be quiet, freckle face. I don't think either one of us will be using the computer today. I think it's broken."

"Get out of the way and let me try," I said. "Let someone try who actually knows what they're doing!"

I pressed the button once, twice, and then three times. Still, it wouldn't turn on. I unplugged the computer and tried plugging it in again.

Still no luck.

"Told ya," Katie said. "Looks like the shrimp can't fix it either."

I had the worst luck ever. The computer had crashed, and I knew zero facts about dinosaurs. My only hope was to see if Mom could drive me to Nana O'Banning's house. Her computer always worked. But Mom wouldn't be home for more than an hour. She had one of those goofy teacher meetings.

My day had taken a nosedive.

I stomped upstairs and flopped down on my bed.

At least I had time to get out my sketchbook and draw for a while. I slid out my pencil box from under my bed and chose a handful of colored pencils.

I imagined I was a famous paleontologist digging in the desert for dinosaur bones. It was so hot that I had to eat ice cream every minute. I drew a picture of myself with a Popsicle in one hand and a shovel in the other.

Then I don't know what came over me.

Underneath the rock, I sketched myself next to the scariest T. rex ever. It was screaming so loudly that it was blowing the pencil right out of my picture-perfect ponytail. As I looked into its huge pink mouth, I could count every one of its pointy teeth. I freaked myself out so much that my hand froze around my pencil. I think that's the mark of a good artist.

"Hey, snap out of it!" said Katie, suddenly. She was always poking her head into my room for no good reason. "You look like you've seen a ghost or something."

For once, I was glad that my sister had opened her big mouth.

I decided to use my eraser and change a few things in my drawing. Instead of making the dinosaur look scary, I colored him purple and drew a propeller hat on his head. I even shared my Popsicle with him. I doubt that dinosaurs were purple or that they ate Popsicles. But it was my secret sketchbook and I could do whatever I wanted. Just when I was about to draw another dinosaur, I heard Mom coming up the stairs. Finally!

"Hey, Chan. You sure got home from school quickly. Katie said that the computer crashed again. I'm sorry about that."

"Yeah, and if you ask me, Katie messed it up. She never waits for the little hourglass thingy to finish. She just clicks and clicks and clicks!" I said. "Can you take me to Nana's? I really need to use her computer. I'm working on a big project—a top secret one!"

"Wow, sounds important," she said. "I need to stop by Nana's anyway. We're having a bake sale at school and I need her help on a few things."

"Thanks, Mom!" I said, especially excited about the bake sale part. "Can she make those triple chunk chocolate cookies this time? Those things are delish! I could eat a dozen in five minutes."

"I'll have to agree with you," Mom said. "But don't let Teeny find out. You know they're his favorite. If that crazy pig gets ahold of them, there won't be a crumb left!"

5

Surfing the Wave

I could hardly wait to get to Nana's house. Whenever I'm upset, I always grab my sketchbook and go to the Secret Artist Hangout. It's my favorite room in her entire house. From construction paper to finger paints, she has everything tucked away into little plastic bins on a shelf. It's an art kid's dream!

Actually, Nana and I are a lot alike. We both love artsy things, we both love chocolate, and of course, we both love Teeny—the coolest pig on the planet. Drawing with Nana always makes me feel better. I once got so upset over bombing a math test that all I wanted to do was draw black clouds and lightning bolts. But when I got an A+ on a book report,

Nana and I celebrated by drawing butterflies and ice cream cones with my Rockin' Red pencil. It was awesome!

Even Teeny gets in on the action every now and then. Nana and I can't quit laughing when he slobbers all over his Piggy Pink pencil. Although I named the pencil after him, all Teeny can do is make a few weird marks on paper.

But the Secret Artist Hangout would have to wait this time. I had some serious web surfing to do. One way or another, I'd figure out what kind of dinosaur was buried at the school playground. I also had a poster to work on for Mr. Reese's class. I didn't mind doing research on dinosaurs, but didn't Mr. Reese know that I had more important things to do than read about boring Native American art?

As we pulled into Nana's driveway, Teeny was waiting for me on the front porch. He bounced up and down, holding a green pencil between his teeth. Green drool dripped down his chin.

I love that crazy pig.

"Looks like he's been expecting you, Chan," Mom said. "That is one strange pig."

"That is one *adorable* pig!" I corrected her.

"Hey there, you two!" said Nana, opening the front door. "I hear you're having computer problems at home. Well, you've come to the right place. I've already got it turned on so you can surf the wave!"

Sometimes Nana acted a little kooky.

"Remember, Nana? It's called surfing the web, not the wave," I giggled. "Thanks for letting me use your computer. I'm on a top-secret mission!"

"Top secret, huh? Can you give me a hint?"

"Nope, my lips are sealed!" I said. "But if I solve this mystery, everyone in Greenville will hear about it."

Teeny oinked loudly and ran around in circles.

"Sorry, Teeny, but I can't tell you either," I joked. "You might squeal and tell everyone in town."

"Then get to it!" Nana said, smiling. "Your mom and I have some planning to do of our own."

I logged on to the computer and typed in my password: COB (for Channing O'Banning). Then I searched "digging for dinosaurs in Greenville."

Zilch. The only results were advertisements about dinosaur exhibits in museums.

I needed a website to help me *find* a dinosaur myself—one that might just end up in a museum. I'd be the most popular kid in town if I discovered the first one!

Then I typed, "Where have dinosaurs been found in America?"

One website said that they'd been discovered in thirty-five states! With those kinds of odds, chances are I had to be on to something. I tried to think about the mysterious rock that we'd already uncovered. Part of it was gray and bumpy, and part of it was white and smooth.

"Any luck on whatever you're looking for, Chan?" asked Nana. "Remember, I have a ton of books on that shelf over there. I've had some of them since your dad was a kid."

"I'll look, Nana, but I doubt I'll find anything. Thanks anyway."

I glanced over at the shelf and saw books on sewing, gardening, and even one called *Golfing for Grannies*. But just as I was ready to give up and go back to the computer, I noticed a book on the bottom shelf. The dusty old book was called *Prehistoric Creatures That Roamed the Earth*.

Victory!

It had tons of dinosaur drawings inside. I studied each one carefully. I never knew so many kinds of dinosaurs roamed the earth. From the spiky-backed ankylosaurus to the triple-horned triceratops, there were dinosaurs of every shape and size.

But as I flipped through the old pages, one dinosaur stood out more than others: the stegosaurus. It had a large hump with sharp things sticking up on its back. It was smooth in some places and bumpy in others—*just like the fossil at school*! I quickly drew the stegosaurus in my sketchbook with my Chocolaty Chip Brown pencil.

"We're finding some yummy recipes in the kitchen," Mom said, popping into the living room. "Want to help us bake, or are you still working on the big mystery?"

"I'm getting closer, Mom. Getting closer!" I said, concentrating on my sketch. "But you guys go ahead and start baking. I'm starving!"

———

"So, if you're not going to tell us about the big secret, let's hear about the big poster that's due soon," said Nana. "What's it about?"

Nana set out a giant plate of chocolate chunk cookies that were still warm.

"Naytif Amurcan arf," I managed to garble with my mouth stuffed full of chocolate yumminess. I swallowed and continued. "Native American art, I mean. Mr. Reese assigned me to do a poster all about it. At least I get to do something about art, I guess."

Nana got so excited that she almost jumped out of her sneakers.

"Well, great gorillas! You have a cousin who lives out West, and she collects all sorts of pottery. I'm sure some of the pots are made by Native Americans! How weird is that?"

"Weird. Very weird," I admitted. "But, Nana, it's not like pottery is real art or anything. And why didn't anyone tell me that I had a cousin out West?"

"Maybe you need to read more about Native American pottery," said Nana. "Art comes in all sorts of forms. Each tribe makes their own unique style of pots, and they're a sight to behold! As for your cousin, Lyndsey, she's your great-aunt Lois's daughter. She moved to New Mexico when you were just a baby."

I was so confused. I'd never met a Lyndsey *or* a Lois, for that matter.

"The last time I heard from Lyndsey, she was dating a young man who works at a museum. Maybe I'll send her a z-mail."

"It's e-mail, Nana, *e-mail*. Not z-mail," I reminded her for the tenth time. "But I doubt that Lyndsey even knows I exist."

"Oh, fiddle faddle. Sure she does," Nana insisted. "She's never met you, but family is family. Once an O'Banning, always an O'Banning! Come to think of it, she sent me a gift last year that you might like to see."

Nana quickly went into her bedroom. *What on earth can she be up to this time?*

Soon she came out holding a small velvet box. Inside was the most beautiful ring I'd ever seen. There was a square turquoise stone in the middle and a tiny silver leaf on the side.

"It's beautiful, Nana!" I said. "Did a Native American make it?"

"I believe so. Many of the tribes in New Mexico are wonderful jewelry artists. Would you like to try it on?"

"Really?" I asked. "Are you sure?"

I slowly slipped the ring onto my pointer finger. It was a perfect fit! I rushed to the mirror and held my hand up to my face.

"See, it just fits," said Nana. "Would you like to wear it to school tomorrow?"

Huh? Is she serious?

"Are you sure, Nana?" I asked. "Are you double *triple* sure?"

"I'm double, triple, *quadruple* sure, Chan. Since you're studying about the Wild West, I think it's perfect timing."

I couldn't believe it. Tomorrow I was wearing something to school made by a real Native American!

"I'll take good care of your ring, Nana," I promised. "Maddy will go crazy when she sees it!"

Tomorrow was going to be full of surprises. From showing off my turquoise ring to giving my stegosaurus dinosaur news to Maddy and Cooper, it was going to be the best day of all time!

6

The Woman Who Loves Horses

I couldn't wait to get to school.

I put on my favorite striped hoodie for good luck and stuck my Totally Turquoise pencil into my ponytail. It was the perfect pencil for my big news.

As a finishing touch, I slipped Nana's turquoise ring onto my finger.

"Are you and your friends going to dig at recess today, Chan?" asked Mom at breakfast. "When are you ever going to tell us what you're up to?"

"Sooner than you think!" I said, chomping on an apple. "This is gonna be big! I mean really big!"

Maddy and Cooper just didn't know it yet. I double-checked my sketchbook to make sure I had my dinosaur drawing.

"What's gonna be big?" asked Katie. She pranced into the kitchen and grabbed the apple right out of my hand.

"Nothing," I insisted. Sometimes Katie could be such a blabbermouth. "Is it okay if I go on to school, Mom?"

I needed to hurry before Katie bugged the answer out of me.

"Sure, just don't forget your shovel," said Mom.

Katie looked more confused than ever.

I grabbed my backpack and raced out the door before the Snoop could ask any more questions.

When I got to school, I searched everywhere for Cooper and Maddy. I even ran out and looked for them at the dig site first, but they were nowhere to be found.

I was bummed. It was just my luck that those two were late for school. Of all the days to be tardy, this was not it.

I hung up my jacket in my locker and slid the stegosaurus drawing into my back pocket. *What if Maddy and Cooper aren't coming to school today? That would totally stink!*

When the bell finally rang, I had no choice but to go to class. My big surprise would have to wait. At least Mr. Reese would make class fun.

"Today is a very special day," said my teacher, smiling. "In a moment you're going to meet a Native American, and you can ask her any question that you'd like."

Awesome! I wondered if our visitor would be wearing a headband full of feathers or bring a bow and arrow to class. Cooper would go bonkers—that is, if he ever made it to class.

After what seemed like forever, my best friends finally marched through the door.

"It's about time you two got here!" I hissed. "Where were you?"

"Don't blame me," Cooper whispered back. "Mom overslept and blamed it on her clock. Then she just *had* to stop and get her drive-through coffee, of all things."

"Yeah, and they almost forgot to pick me up too!" Maddy added. "But it sounds like we got here just in time. I can't believe we get to meet a real Native American!"

Soon we heard a knock on the door, and Mr. Reese welcomed the visitor inside. She looked about the same age as Nana but with darker skin and long black hair. I couldn't help but notice her turquoise and silver necklace. It had a turquoise flower in the center and silver beads on each side. It was almost as pretty as Nana's ring. *Almost.*

"Class, this is Pelipa Smith," said Mr. Reese. "She's from the Zuni tribe we've been studying about. Pelipa is in town visiting her grandson. Can everyone say hello?"

"Hi, Pelipa," everyone said.

"*Keshi,*" said our visitor. "That means 'hello' in Zuni. Even though my family speaks English, many of us speak Zuni as well."

"Do any of you have any questions for Pelipa?" asked Mr. Reese.

Maddy, Cooper, and I looked over at one another and froze. We didn't have a clue what to ask. But then Maddy thought of something at the very same time that I did. She beat me to it by raising her hand.

"My name is Madison. What does *Pelipa* mean?"

That's exactly what I was going to ask!

"That's a good question," Pelipa said. "In my culture, *Pelipa* means 'lover of horses.' All of our names have special meanings, and horses were very important to our people. Pelipa is a normal name for us, just like Madison is a normal name for your family."

"There is *nothing* normal about Maddy!" Cooper joked.

"Cooper Newberry," said Mr. Reese, "I think you should remember that we have a visitor and to mind your manners."

Cooper sunk so far down in his seat that I could only see the top of his head.

"Do you live in a tepee, Miss Pelipa?" I asked. "You know, like the Native Americans do on TV?"

"No, I don't live in one of those," she said nicely. "Members of the Apache tribe used to live in tepees long ago, though. I live in a house just like most of you. Some of my people still live in adobe houses, however. They're called pueblos. Some have lived there for many years. If fact, many tribes such as Zuni, Hopi, and Acoma are even referred to as Pueblo people."

I knew what a pueblo was! Mr. Reese had shown us in our social studies book. They look like huge, dusty rectangles stacked on top of one another to make one big stone city. I'd even drawn one in my sketchbook.

"Miss Pelipa?" I asked, raising my hand again. "Where did you get your necklace? It's really cool."

"Well, thank you . . . what's your name?" she asked.

"Channing O'Banning," I said quietly. "I like turquoise rocks a lot."

"So that's why you like my necklace," she said. "I like turquoise too. My grandfather, Lonan, made it for me when I was a little girl. His name means 'Clouds.' I think of him whenever I wear it because turquoise looks like the sky."

That's when I decided to try to get Maddy's attention and show her my ring. But when I looked down at my hand, the most terrible thing *ever* happened.

Nana's ring was not on my finger.

It was gone! How could that be?

I looked around my desk and even in my book bag. Perhaps it had slid off of my finger or something.

But it was no use. It wasn't there. I suddenly didn't feel so good and my stomach hurt. Maddy and Cooper could tell something was wrong.

I'd wanted to ask Pelipa more questions, but now all I could think of was Nana's ring. But Cooper made up for it. He had a zillion questions for Pelipa.

She went on to tell us how corn was very important to her people and that many of her ancestors traded jewelry with other tribes. If I were a Zuni, I'd trade almost anything for turquoise. I'd trade in *all* of my pencils if I could find Nana's ring. I'd even trade Katie the Snoop if I could. That would be a no-brainer.

After Pelipa finished answering questions, the bell rang for recess. It was almost time to tell Cooper and Maddy my big news. I could hardly wait to show them my drawing. Maddy might scream so loudly that she'd crack the windows in the library. Cooper might even faint. I just wished I wasn't so worried about Nana's missing ring so I could focus on being excited with them.

7

The Worst Day of My Stinky Life

When the bell rang, we were the first kids on the playground. Cooper had the shovels and paintbrushes in his backpack and got ready to start digging. I was still upset over losing Nana's ring, and I told my friends about losing it while we got our supplies out. They were both sure it would turn up, but I wasn't so sure. I hoped sharing my news about the dinosaur would make me feel better. I got a little nervous and my palms got sticky.

"Think we'll uncover anything new today?" asked Cooper. He got on his hands and knees and began brushing away pebbles.

"We've still got a lot of digging to do," Maddy said. "Chan, did you ask your dad what he thought might be under here? Since he's a doctor, maybe he can help."

"He takes care of patients, not rocks," Cooper joked. "Right, Chan?"

This was my chance. I took a deep breath and reached into my back pocket.

"Uh, Maddy, Cooper, I think I know what's under there," I said quickly. "I did some research on the computer last night."

Both of them stopped digging and threw down their shovels.

"I think we're digging up a stegosaurus!" I said and quickly showed them my sketch I drew from Nana's book.

Maddy's eyes got as big as ping-pong balls.

"A what-a-saurus?" she asked, not believing what I'd said.

"Really? A stegosaurus?" asked Cooper, jerking the sketch from my hand. "Do you *really* think that's what it is?"

"It's gotta be!" I said bravely, pointing to my sketch. "It has the big humps on its back and it's smooth in other places. It looks just like what we're digging!"

"Wow, you're right! You're a genius, Channing O'Banning!" screamed Cooper. "You're a dinosaur-drawing genius!"

Maddy jumped up and down and gave me a hug. We all high-fived one another and did a victory dance.

This is the best day ever!

"Our principal will probably call the newspaper as soon as she hears about it," I said. "They might even print my drawing of the stegosaurus on the front page. This is gonna be *b-i-g*!"

"They'll probably take our photo," said Maddy. "I hope they'll wait until tomorrow because I'm having a bad hair day."

"We'll probably be on TV too!" Cooper said. "Channing O'Banning, you're the best!"

"Yeah, you're the best," Maddy agreed. "We gotta finish digging, and fast!"

We brushed away pebbles as fast as we could and were almost at the bottom of the hole. I could already imagine how I'd pose for the photographers. Mom might even buy me a new pair of high-top sneakers. Or better yet, a new set of colored pencils. And I bet I could buy Nana a whole drawer of turquoise rings when I was rich and famous for discovering a real dinosaur fossil.

That is, until Katie and her sixth grade friends came by.

"Whatcha doing, squirt?" Katie asked, trying to show off to her friends.

"None of your business," I said quickly. I wasn't ready to tell her my big news. "Why don't you go hang out somewhere else."

But my snoop of a sister totally ignored me.

"Let's see, what do we have here? Shovels and . . . paintbrushes? What are you kids up to?"

I held my breath, hoping my friends wouldn't tell her anything. I crossed my fingers for extra luck.

"We might as well tell you," squealed Maddy. "We've discovered a dinosaur!"

"A stegosaurus to be exact," Cooper interrupted. "It's probably the biggest thing to ever happen at Greenville Elementary!"

"A *what*?" asked Katie. "Yeah, right. You three are such babies."

Katie's friend Andrea moved in to take a closer look.

"There's not a dinosaur down there," Andrea laughed, looking into the hole.

"Sure there is!" said Cooper. "You're just jealous because you didn't discover it."

Cooper was right. He was the only one brave enough to say it.

"I'm not jealous over a big heap of concrete," said Andrea.

"Huh?" I asked. "Concrete?"

Perhaps I was hearing things.

"There used to be some monkey bars here," Katie said. "But after Lilly Hoffman fell off and broke her arm, the principal had the monkey bars removed. This heap of concrete is the only thing left."

Katie bent over and laughed her head off. So did her friends.

I wanted to find a closet and hide.

"Concrete?" said Maddy. I could tell that my BFF was totally disappointed. She looked sadder than the day her mom told her no to that poodle she asked for last year. "Are you serious, Katie?"

"I'm positive," said the Snoop. "Maybe one of these days you kids will grow up."

I felt horrible. I wished my sister didn't exist! "Go away, Katie!" I screamed. I'm sure every kid on the playground heard me. "You always ruin *everything*!"

"So much for this being the biggest thing to happen at school," Cooper sighed. "It's more like the most embarrassing thing ever."

It was all my fault.

"We did all of this work for nothing. This is the worst day in the history of worst days," Maddy said sadly.

"I'm so sorry, guys," I whispered in shock, lowering my head. But I don't think they even heard me. They were too busy picking up their shovels and paintbrushes.

If only I could go home and hide in my room forever. *I can never show my face in fourth grade again. And how can I ever go back to my Nana's house after losing her turquoise ring? My days at the Secret Artist Hangout are over too.*

Perhaps I should leave town and join a traveling circus? Maybe Teeny can go too, and we'll do crazy pet tricks. He can snort his ABCs, after all.

But what am I thinking? If my grandmother can't even trust me with her most special ring, she certainly will not let me leave Greenville with the most wonderful pig on earth.

I should have known all along that this whole digging thing was a total waste of time. And even worse, it was also a total waste of my good colored pencils!

8

Nana Knows Best

As I walked home from school I noticed that Nana's car was in the driveway. How would I ever tell her that I'd lost the most special ring she owned? I dreaded going inside, but maybe Teeny was with her. He always understood. Then again, he never did say anything to the contrary.

"Hey, Teeny," I said, giving him a hug as he raced to the door. He was covered in flour from head to hoof.

It was easy to tell that Mom and Nana were baking cookies. The house smelled just like a bakery. But for once, I didn't feel like eating. I was too sad about losing Nana's ring. *How am I ever going to tell her?*

"You're just in time to wash the dishes!" Nana joked. Flour dotted her eyeglasses, and I doubt she could see much of anything.

"Hi, Nana," I said sadly, looking down at the ground. I fed Teeny a gummy turtle.

"Only give him one. I'm making cupcakes next, and he'll go wild over those too. Heaven knows that crazy pig has a sweet tooth!"

Mom came into the kitchen and put her arm around me. "I have a feeling that someone needs a hug today."

I could tell that Mom already knew about my stupid dinosaur idea. I'm sure Katie the Big Mouth told the entire school.

"I'm sorry, dear," Mom said. "But don't be so

hard on yourself. The three of you had fun digging outside. Plus, you got some really good drawings for your sketchbook."

I planned on tearing those sketches into a million pieces. I didn't want any reminder of the most embarrassing moment of my life.

"Mom, how can I ever go to school again?" I asked. "They'll laugh me out of fourth grade! Maddy and Cooper probably hate me for convincing them it might be a dinosaur."

"Oh, fiddle faddle!" said Nana, joining the conversation. "That's plain silly. I don't even know what happened at school, but I know Maddy and Cooper. And I know my Channing O'Banning. You guys are like the three musketeers!"

"The *who*?" I asked, confused.

"Oh, never mind," she said. "Just know that it will all work out. Have some faith, Chan! Real friends forgive one another, right? I'm sure both Maddy and Cooper know Ephesians 4:32. You know, how the Bible says we should forgive one another, just like God forgives us?"

"I guess so," I said. But I knew what I had to do next.

"Nana, something else happened at school

today. It's just . . . just . . . horrible! It's all my fault."

I could feel my heart racing in my chest. I didn't want to look up.

"Chan, it can't be *that* bad. Just take a deep breath and tell us. I love you no matter what."

"Nana's right," Mom said. "Whatever it is, we'll work it out."

If only Mom could be right about this. I took a deep breath and spoke as quickly as I could.

"I don't know what happened, Nana, but I sort of lost your turquoise ring. I had it on my finger one minute, and then the next minute it was gone!" I could feel myself starting to cry. "I'm so sorry, Nana. I'm very, very sorry. I know it was your favorite," I cried.

Teeny nudged the tissue box over to me.

"Oh . . . I see," said Nana. "But it's okay, Chan. You didn't mean to lose it. At least you told me the truth. Your honesty means more than any ring. So see, that wasn't so bad, was it?"

"Do you have any idea where you could have lost it?" Mom asked. "You really need to take special care of things, especially when they're not yours."

"I know, Mom, but I don't have a clue where it could be," I said.

"Well, it's over now," Nana said. "Let's just forget

about it. We've got some baking to do! How about helping us, Chan?"

I felt so much better after telling Nana the truth about the whole thing.

"Can I help decorate some of the cookies?" I asked. "The snowflakes are my favorite."

"Okay, but only if you've done your homework," Mom said. "I spoke with Mr. Reese about your assignment."

Sometimes it was a real bummer having a mom who was also a teacher at my school.

"I did most of my homework in class. Can't I just decorate one cookie? *Please?*" I said, using my puppy dog pout. That usually worked.

"Only one," Mom warned. "And then I believe someone has a poster to work on. Isn't that right?"

Great gorillas! Did Mr. Reese have to tell Mom *everything*? I guess one cookie was better than none. I got the tube of white icing and made all sorts of swirls on the cookie. Then I grabbed a handful of sparkly blue sugar and sprinkled it on the top. It was almost too pretty to eat.

"You're definitely the artist of the family," said Nana. "That cookie is a work of art! Snowflakes are my favorite too. They remind me of how different we all are. Just think of you and your friends. Cooper likes science, Maddy loves ballet, and you like doing anything artsy. What a blessing it is that God made us all so unique."

"You can say that again!" said the Snoop, entering the kitchen. "If there were two of Channing O'Banning, we'd all go crazy!"

Great. I loved it when my sister came home early. *Not.*

9

Pack Your Bags

Something weird was going on.

Very weird.

Dad was usually home and helped me with my homework. I was counting on his help with the poster assignment.

"Where's Dad?" I asked at dinner.

"Sometimes a really sick patient comes in and it takes more time," Mom explained. "Or perhaps he's straightening up the waiting room. The little ones can sure make a mess of the magazines."

"Can I run next door and check?" I asked. "Maybe he'll let me help clean up."

"Sure, Chan. And tell him dinner's getting cold."

Dad once paid me three dollars for straightening

up the magazines in the waiting room. I could really use the money right now. I'd decided to buy Nana a new turquoise ring. It was the least I could do after losing the other one.

But I had no idea where I could find a turquoise ring in Greenville. I thought about digging for turquoise in my backyard. Maybe I'd get lucky. But one thing was for sure: I would never dig for anything at school ever again!

As I opened the door to Dad's office, I could hear him on the phone with someone. "That's wonderful news!" he said. "Congratulations to both of you! We'll be in touch soon."

What good news? I sure don't know of any.

"Hey, Chan, what a surprise," Dad smiled. "Are you here for a checkup?"

"No way!" I said, giggling. "I thought I'd come over and see if you needed any help. Oh yeah, and Mom said dinner's getting cold."

"Hmm. I don't think I need any help at the moment, but thanks for offering," Dad said. "By any chance, are you trying to raise money for something?"

Double darn it! Dad knew me too well. I didn't want to tell him the whole story of why I needed money, but I had no choice. As Dad finished cleaning, I told him about the whole nightmare. I started with the dig disaster and ended with the loss of Nana's ring.

"That's too bad," said Dad. "But at least you were honest with her. Even when it's hard, it's really important to tell the truth. On second thought, I'm sure there are a few odd jobs that your mom or I can find for you. You can always help wash the dinner dishes, and perhaps you can make sure to keep your room clean each day. That way I can pay you your full allowance and not just half of it."

Ugh. Drying dishes was my least favorite chore ever. But I knew I needed the money and that Mom could use my help—especially after a long day of teaching. And I guess Dad's right about my room, even though I hate to admit it. My bed would probably look a lot neater if I made it up every morning.

"Thanks, Dad, I'll try to do both of those things. I'll also have plenty of time to help on Saturdays if you need me. I'm sure Cooper and Maddy won't ever ask me to hang out with them again. I kind of embarrassed them at school today."

"Oh, I wouldn't be so sure," Dad said, trying to make me feel better. "Just give it some time. Winter break starts next week, and I have a surprise for everyone!"

"Really?" I asked. "A surprise? Does it have anything to do with that phone call? You sure were smiling."

"As a matter of fact, it does," he said. "But right now, I'm starving. I'll race you!"

Dad took off like a rocket, running out the door toward the house. I quickly rushed past him, jumped over three steps, and made it through the kitchen door just in time. Whew!

"Great gorillas!" Nana said. "You caused me to break the head off of a gingerbread man!"

"That means I can eat it!" Dad joked, reaching from behind me to grab the cookie. "You win, Chan, fair and square. Now go tell everyone to come to the kitchen."

"Is anyone going to tell me what in the world is going on?" Mom asked.

I could hardly wait myself. I needed some good news after having the yuckiest day in the universe.

"The reason I'm getting home late is because I received a call from our cousin Lyndsey."

"Lyndsey?" asked Nana. "Channing, that's my niece that I was telling you about. Well, I'll be a monkey's uncle!"

"You mean a piggy's Nana," Katie joked. "What did Lyndsey have to say, Dad?"

"She's getting married next week. Even though it's short notice, she'd like us to come to the wedding."

"Sweet!" I shouted. "But doesn't she live out West? Are we really going out West, Dad?"

"Yeah, can we go?" asked Katie. "We've never been out there before. I'll even be nice to Chan if we can go. Well, uh, I'll try."

"Count me in too," said Nana. "I'd love to see that part of the country again."

"Since it's winter break, and since we haven't seen her in a long time, I say we go for it," Dad announced.

"Yes!" Katie and I yelled at the same time. I think it's the only thing we've agreed on in five years.

Even Teeny jumped up and down. It almost looked like he was smiling, from one pointy ear to the other.

What a goofy pig!

10

The Wild, Wild West!

I could hardly wait for the plane to land in New Mexico. I'd never been to the Southwest and could only imagine what it was like. I remembered the pictures of rocky landforms that Boring Doring had shown us in class. Some of the canyons were orange, red, yellow, and everything in between. They looked like something on another planet. I could hardly wait to see them in real life!

I passed the time by doing a Wild West drawing in my sketchbook. I imagined that Teeny and Nana were riding in a covered wagon like people did long ago. Mr. Reese said that everyone traveled along the Santa Fe Trail and that the roads used to be made of dirt. Talk about a bumpy ride!

I also drew a picture of a Native American and pretended it was me. I wore a shirt made out of buffalo hide and drew a turkey feather in my ponytail. Maybe I was from the Zuni tribe? Or the Apache? Since it was my sketchbook, I could do whatever I wanted.

Teeny slept the whole way on the plane. He only woke up to eat five bags of pretzels that the flight attendant had given him.

I couldn't quit thinking about Maddy and Cooper. They didn't even know I was going to New Mexico. I doubt they'd miss me anyway. That dumb stegosaurus ended up being a concrete-a-saurus and a stink-o-saurus.

Maybe I'll hide out in a pueblo.

As we were descending for landing, I looked out

the plane window. I could see red rocks and cacti everywhere, just like in my drawing! But when we finally landed, all I could see was a bunch of buildings. What a bummer.

So much for the Wild West.

Katie was surprised too.

"Hey, where's all the cowboy and Indian stuff you told me about?" Katie asked me. "I should have known better than to believe you, Channing O'Banning. Or should I say *dino-girl!*"

If only I could put a zipper on Katie's mouth. Sometimes she could be downright mean.

"This part of the country has both cities *and* deserts," said Mom. "That's what makes it so unique. Just wait. You'll see!"

"There they are!" said Nana, pointing to the waiting area.

My cousin Lyndsey and her fiancé, Miguel, were holding a poster that said Welcome, O'Banning Gang!

"My, my, Lyndsey's all grown up," said Nana. "She's so beautiful!"

"And her fiancé is a hunka munka!" blurted Katie.

"Okay, cool it, Katie O'Banning," Mom warned. "Time to calm down."

Katie could be such a weirdo.

After we exchanged hugs and introduced them

to Teeny, my stomach started grumbling as usual. I was so embarrassed.

"Sounds like someone's hungry," said Lyndsey. "Do you like Mexican food? I know a great place close by."

"Can we go, Dad?" I asked. I could almost taste the chips and salsa. "You know how much I love tacos!"

"Sure," said Dad. "I'm starving too. It must run in the family."

"Channing, maybe you can show me some of your drawings while we're waiting on our food. Nana says you're a wonderful artist."

Yikes.

I wasn't so sure that I wanted to show Lyndsey and Miguel my sketchbook. *What if they hate my drawings?*

But before I knew it, Teeny pranced over to us, holding my sketchbook in his mouth. It fell to the floor, and my stegosaurus drawing just happened to fall out.

Uh-oh.

"Wow," said Lyndsey. "That's a wonderful drawing of a dinosaur!"

I felt the color drain from my face. I did not feel like talking about the you-know-what. But, of course, Katie had to laugh out loud at me like her typical bratty self. She knew *exactly* what I was thinking.

"Oh, uh, thanks, Lyndsey," I said, grabbing my sketch and slapping my sketchbook closed. "I was just doodling one day, that's all."

"I like to doodle and draw as well," said Miguel. "Any reason you chose the stegosaurus?"

But before I could answer, Katie had to open her big mouth.

"I can tell you why!" she said. "You see, it all started back on the playground at school. And Channing thought . . ."

But just as Katie was about to embarrass me for life, Teeny hopped up on her lap and knocked over her soda. My big sister was soaked from head to toe.

I wanted to kiss that clumsy pig.

"Teeny shouldn't be allowed in restaurants!" Katie said, stomping off to the bathroom. "He doesn't even like tacos!"

"I just like to draw dinosaurs a lot," I told Miguel and Lyndsey. Thanks goodness Katie was in the bathroom. My cousin didn't need to know about my dingbat dinosaur idea.

"Excellent!" said Miguel. "I like them too. Would you like to see some real dinosaurs, or at least a cool exhibit of their bones?"

"Really?" I asked. "I'd love to!"

"Count us in too," said Dad, motioning to the rest of the gang.

Teeny squealed so loudly that we had to cover our ears. I guess that meant yes for him too.

"Did I mention that Miguel just happens to be the curator at the natural history museum? We can go after lunch, if you'd like," Lyndsey said as she put her arm around Miguel, which made him blush as pink as Teeny.

"Yes!" I squealed. "But what's a curator? I've never heard of one of those."

"Good question, Chan," Mom said. "A curator is someone who organizes and oversees the exhibits at a museum. They get to look at all sorts of interesting things, including different kinds of art."

"Then I'm going to be a curator when I grow up," I said. "That sounds like the best job ever!"

I could hardly wait to see the dinosaur bones. I wondered which ones were on display. Anything would be better than staring at a big heap of concrete.

The natural history museum in New Mexico was incredible! Not only did they have stegosaurus, T.rex, triceratops, and pterodactyl bones, but it looked like they were alive. Sound effects played in the background so it seemed as if they were actually roaring.

I was a little scared, but I tried to remind myself that it was just a big heap of bones.

As we walked to the next display, a large sign caused me to stop in my tracks. A big blue arrow pointed the way to Turquoise Mine Exhibit.

Yes! Maybe I can find a piece of turquoise for Nana's ring!

As I walked through the exhibit, I saw every step turquoise goes through to become a beautiful stone. It goes from being a plain-looking rock to a shiny blue mineral.

But even as I was learning about one of the coolest things ever, I remembered I had a job to do.

"Cousin Lyndsey, do you know where I can buy a turquoise ring? I need to buy a gift for someone special," I whispered.

"Sure, Chan. There are tons of stores in Santa Fe that sell turquoise jewelry. But I gotta warn you: it can be very expensive."

Expensive was not the word that I wanted to hear. I probably couldn't even afford a turquoise ring! I'd done everything to earn extra money—from waking up early to make my bed, to helping Mom wash the dinner dishes three nights in a row. One day I even made Katie's bed for a dollar. She said it was worth every penny for me to act like "her little maid." Ugh.

If I still didn't have enough money, that meant I'd made the Snoop's messy bed for nothing.

What a rip-off!

I decided to look at the rings in the museum gift shop. But Lyndsey was right—they were way too expensive. And it was too late to earn any more money.

"Just be patient, Chan. We have plenty of time," Mom said. "It's time to go check in to our hotel. It's a real adobe, by the way. Didn't you just study about that in school?"

Mom was right. But I'd never heard of an adobe hotel. *Weird. Very weird.*

Mr. Reese would think it was totally cool. Maybe I'd draw it in my sketchbook and show him when I got back.

We had three days left in New Mexico. Surely I could find Nana a ring by then.

As Dad drove north to Santa Fe, we saw the snow-covered mountains and the colorful desert. Mom even pointed to a great horned sheep grazing high on a mountain. Its horns curled backward and it looked like it was wearing a wig.

"Hey, it sort of looks like you, Chan!" joked Katie.

So much for my sister trying to be nice.

"Oh, you're *so* funny," I said. "Maybe we can find your twin out here—a big-toothed gopher!"

"Okay, that's enough, girls," Mom said. "Why don't you look out the window at the scenery? Isn't it just beautiful? I can see why the Zuni live here."

Zuni! I'd almost forgotten! I still had that poster to do for Mr. Reese's class. It was due as soon as I got back, and I didn't have a clue where to start. But I was in luck—I was in the land of the Zuni. So I decided that I needed to find a member of the Zuni tribe—and fast!

But honestly, I had no idea where to even start looking.

11

Santa Fe Surprise

Mom was right. Our hotel *was* a real adobe! The outside was an orangey brown color that looked like clay. The inside had smooth walls with woven rugs on the floors. Katie and I had a room next to Nana's, and it even had a fireplace called a *kiva*. I flopped down onto my bed and got out my sketchbook. I drew a rug with all sorts of lines, zigzags, and swirls. Luckily I had the perfect pencil, Jelly Bean Black, in my ponytail. After finishing my sketch and unpacking my suitcase, I noticed something strange. Beside our bed hung a weird leather circle, woven like a spiderweb. It had long strands of beads that hung from the bottom.

"Hey, Katie, what is this thing?" I asked, touching the beads.

"Beats me. Maybe it's some sort of animal trap. Have you seen the size of the lizards around here? They're ginormous!"

"That's a dumb idea, Katie," I said, looking at the leather thing more closely. "It has holes in it. I don't think it's a lizard trap."

As I was still trying to figure it out, Teeny and Nana came over to check out our room.

"Hey, no fair, you girls have a dream catcher!" said Nana.

"A *what*?" Katie asked.

"Is that what this thing is?" I asked, holding it up.

"Many tribes believe that a dream catcher catches all the bad dreams you have at night and only lets through the good ones. Not a bad idea, if you ask me."

"You said it, Nana," Katie replied. "They must know that I have to sleep with Chan on this vacation. Now that's a real nightmare!"

"Oh, yeah? Well, they probably know that you snore like a train and felt sorry for me. There isn't a dream catcher big enough to catch your motor mouth!"

"Okay, okay, time to behave," Nana warned. "It's pretty bad when Teeny behaves better than you two."

I gave Katie the meanest look I could. Maybe we could drop her off in the mountains with the big-horn sheep.

"Now that we've all rested a bit, how about we do a little exploring?" asked Dad, poking his head into our room.

"I read that they have lots of art galleries here," Mom said, winking at me. "The Native Americans sell their pottery and jewelry here also."

"Sounds great!" I grabbed my allowance money and stuffed it into my pocket.

"Sounds horrible," Katie said. "Who wants to look in a bunch of boring old art galleries?"

Why did Katie have to ruin everything? Why did we have to bring her along in the first place? Teeny was way more fun than my grouchy sister.

"Oh, come on, Katie," said Nana. "You might actually have fun and learn a little something."

"Where are we going first?" I asked. "Are you sure that Native Americans really live around here?"

"I'm sure," said Dad. "Lyndsey told me about places to visit. There's even a pueblo where Native Americans have lived for more than one thousand years. It's in a town called Taos. Maybe we'll go there too."

"Awesome! We studied about that in social studies class!"

"Then off we go," Mom said. "After all, you have a poster due when you get home."

Ugh! Why did she have to remind me?

12

Shop Till You Drop

Mom and Lyndsey were right. There were tons of art galleries in Santa Fe. I kept a pencil in my ponytail and my sketchbook out at all times. One of the stores sold rugs similar to the ones in our hotel. Many were made by the Apache, Cherokee, and even the Navajo!

"Wow, these rugs are awesome, huh, Mom?" I asked. "Every single one looks totally different from the others."

"They're works of art, that's for sure. I read in a brochure that many of the rugs actually tell a story," Mom explained. "Each symbol has a special meaning to the artist who creates it. Lots of hard work and long hours go into weaving them. Just look at all these different colors. Magnificent!"

I never thought of rugs as art before, but now it made sense. They were sort of like my sketchbook. When I create a drawing, it's usually for an important reason. Nana still has the drawing I made for her fiftieth birthday on her refrigerator. I'm sure Native American kids create special things for their family and friends too.

"Oh, I *really* like this one." Mom held up a black and white rug with a man and woman woven in the center.

"You have good taste," said the store owner, walking over to Mom. I noticed the wide turquoise bracelet around his wrist and the beautiful turquoise belt around his waist.

"Welcome to my shop. My name is Ashki, and this is a wedding blanket. It's woven by the Navajo to celebrate the joining of two families."

"It's very nice," said Mom. "I'm sure they're very difficult to make."

"It takes months," Ashki said, pointing to the rug. "Here is the bride, the groom, and even their family and animals."

This was too much of a coincidence for me to pass up.

"Are you thinking what I'm thinking?" I asked Mom.

"I sure am," she said. "This would be the perfect wedding gift for Lyndsey and Miguel."

"Even I like it," said Katie.

"Wow, it's a miracle that you two agree on something!" Dad said.

"I'm delighted that you like the blanket. My cousin is the artist who made this one. We're from the Navajo tribe."

"See, Chan, even designing a rug is a type of art. It takes a lot of talent to make something so beautiful," Mom said.

She was right. There were many kinds of art that I hadn't thought of.

And I couldn't believe that I'd just met someone from the Navajo tribe! I couldn't wait to tell Maddy and Cooper. But then I remembered they probably weren't speaking to me. I tried not to think about it.

In every art gallery we saw something different: rugs, wooden flutes, blankets, and lots of paintings. I wished my art teacher at Greenville could have seen all of this.

"Hey, can we go in this store, Nana?" I asked. "It looks like it has some cool stuff." I crossed my fingers that there was jewelry for sale.

When we walked inside, there were tons of clay

pots of every shape and size. Some had birds painted on them and some had lines going in every direction. I couldn't imagine how they painted such tiny designs on each pot.

"Teeny, don't you dare touch anything in here," warned Nana. "See the sign? It says You Break It, You Buy It. I don't think you have any cash, so *behave*."

Teeny must have known that Nana meant business. He walked quickly over to the corner and sat on his hind legs without the slightest snort.

While I looked around, I couldn't help but think about Mr. Reese and the vase he'd shown us. At that exact moment, I looked up to the top shelf and saw something familiar. There was a whole row of wedding vases! They looked just like Mr. Reese's, only bigger. The one I liked the best had black wavy lines painted on it. The tag said, "Made by Lusita from the Zuni tribe."

"Yes!" I squealed. "Nana, this one is made by a Zuni!"

I quickly drew it in my sketchbook.

A pretty lady with a long black braid came over to check out what I was doing. She looked about Mom's age and wore a colorful dress with a fancy leather belt.

"That's a wonderful sketch," she said nicely. "My name is Elu. My sister, Lusita, made the vase you're drawing."

"I know what kind it is! It's a wedding vase, isn't it? The groom drinks out of one side, and the bride drinks out of the other."

"Very good. You are correct," she said.

"Wow, Chan. I had no idea you knew that," said Nana. "Elu, please tell your sister that she makes beautiful pots."

"Yeah, tell her from me too!"

"Would you like to tell her yourself?" Elu asked. "She's in the back making more pottery. Would you like to see?"

"Sure! Can we, Nana? Please?"

"I don't know why not. I'd like to see that myself. Teeny, stay put. Don't move one hoof!"

We walked toward the back of the store into a small workshop. Lusita was rolling clay into long, skinny pieces. Her creation didn't look anything like a pot.

Weird. Very weird.

"This is how Lusita begins. We call this coil pottery. She puts one coil on top of the other and smoothens them together."

"Hello," said Lusita. "Who do we have here?"

My throat got dry and my tongue froze.

75

"Uh . . . my name is, is uh . . ." I suddenly couldn't remember my own name!

"I'm Channing," I continued. "Channing O'Banning. But you can all me Chan."

"That's a pretty name," she said. "Would you like to help me make a pot?"

Did she just say what I think she said?

"I need someone to roll out the coils. It's sort of like rolling cookie dough into a log. Would you like to try, Chan?" asked Lusita.

Cookie dough? I knew I was a pro at handling cookie dough. This was going to be super easy.

"Sure!" I said, hopping onto a stool. After watching Lusita first, I wet my hands with water and rolled out the clay. It was way harder than it looked. Lusita rounded each coil on top of the other, over and over again, until her creation looked like one long coil. As she formed it into a small pot, she took a little wooden tool and smoothed it all together.

"Now I'll put the pot into my kiln, which is a very, very hot oven. Then I will paint it and heat it all over again. This will make the pot really hard, and it can then be used for all sorts of things."

"Wow, making a pot is a lot harder than it looks!" I said. "And I thought drawing with my colored pencils was tough."

"You're right," said Lusita. "And every pot is different. Every design is just as special as the other."

"Wow, I never thought of it that way," I said.

"It's true, you know," said Nana. "I think I'll buy this one for Lyndsey and Miguel. They'll love knowing that you helped make their wedding vase. Now, if we can just find Teeny. Let's just hope he isn't stuck in a pot, snout first!"

13

The Turquoise Trail

When we met back up with the rest of the gang, I barely recognized Katie. Her blond hair was tucked under a cowboy hat, and on her feet were a pair of sparkly red cowgirl boots. They weren't as cool as my purple high-top sneakers, but they suited my sister perfectly. She must have spent every penny of her allowance on that outfit.

"So much for you thinking that New Mexico was boring!" I reminded her. "Did you get lost in a Wild West clothing store? You fit right in here."

"Yeah, this place is pretty cool," said Katie. "And guess what? The guy who sold us the boots told us about a place where you can dig for turquoise. He even gave us a map."

Wait. What?

"Let's go, let's go! Where is it? Where is it?" I squealed.

My luck might be turning around!

"Calm down," Katie said. "It could be far away, for all I know. But it's on a road called the Turquoise Trail. I guess that's a good sign."

"Sounds like a place worth checking out," Mom said. "Let's all pile into the van and try to find it. You too, Teeny!"

Dad got in the driver's seat, and Mom gave him directions on where to turn. After driving several miles, we finally noticed a sign for the Turquoise Trail.

"There it is! There it is! It says turn right!" I pointed out. "Go there, Dad!"

"Okay, I see it. It's on up ahead," Dad said. "But remember, we have to get back to Santa Fe soon. Lyndsey's wedding is tomorrow."

After driving a little farther on the Turquoise

Trail, we noticed a storefront with a flashing blue sign: Mine Tours Sold Here. My heart started racing.

"Dad, we have to stop! Please!" I begged. "It's a museum too!"

I checked to make sure that I still had my allowance money. This was my best chance yet to find a piece of turquoise for Nana's ring.

Before we could explore the mine, the guide had us watch a video called *The History of Turquoise.*

I don't have time to watch a movie! I have a rock to find!

But it was way more interesting than I'd thought it would be. I even saw pictures of fancy turquoise jewelry worn by Zuni and Hopi princesses.

"I wish I was a Native American princess," I whispered to Katie.

"Yeah, me too," she agreed. "I've never seen jewelry like this before. Not even at the mall."

"Yeah, me neither," I said. "This jewelry is special. Right, Dad?"

"Right, Chan. Many tribes pass their beautiful jewelry down to other family members too."

That reminded me that I'd lost Nana's special ring. I felt horrible all over again.

"Dad, can we go look for turquoise now? Please?"

"Alright, Chan," Dad agreed. "Let's go find that guide."

The mine was huge and hard to climb. I walked around and around, turning over one rock after another. None of the rocks looked like turquoise to me. The guide showed us what to look for, but I couldn't find anything that remotely looked like turquoise. The rocks looked as dull as the ones at school. I looked at rock after rock, trying to find a blue one. Even Teeny tried to help by using his snout to sort through the pebbles.

"Thanks, Teeny, but I'm afraid it's no use," I said, scratching his ear. "This was a crazy idea."

"You can say that again. It's almost as crazy as you trying to dig up that concrete monster at school!" Katie shouted.

"Oh, be quiet, Katie! You're such a—"

But suddenly, out of the corner of my eye, I saw a hint of blue.

Can it be? Can it really, truly be?

I flew past Katie, picked up the rock, and took it to the tour guide.

"Well, I do believe you've found a piece of turquoise!" she said. "See the sky-blue line there? Once it's cut and polished, you'll have a precious little stone."

"Can you cut and polish it here?" I begged. I crossed my fingers and toes. I was running out of time.

"As a matter of fact, we have a jewelry shop that can help you. But it won't be finished until tomorrow."

"Can you make a ring out of it?" I whispered into her ear. I made sure that Nana was nowhere around. "It's a surprise for someone special." I dug around in my pocket and pulled out the few bills I had. "Is this enough money?"

"Since you found your own turquoise stone, this is just enough. And your secret's safe with me," said the tour guide as she winked at me. "I'll even pinky promise to make it official."

"What are you two locking pinkies about?" asked Nana. She had an armful of rocks and looked worn to a frazzle. "I've looked at every one of these crazy rocks and can't find a single thing!"

Nana's glasses were half off and her hair was a mess. "This turquoise hunting is for the birds! Are you *sure* this is a turquoise mine?" she asked. "I'm pooped."

"I'm sure, Nana," I said, giggling at my grandmother. "I'm absolutely sure."

14

Here Comes the Bride

So far, our trip to the Southwest had been one of the best vacations ever. After enjoying everything from looking at dinosaurs to digging in a turquoise mine, I'd decided that New Mexico was my new favorite place. And to top it all off, we were going to Lyndsey and Miguel's wedding. A giant slice of wedding cake was in my future.

Mom rushed Katie and me to get ready, and even had to help Dad with his tie—twice! Nana made sure that the wedding vase was wrapped tightly so it wouldn't break.

"Teeny, if you put one pink hoof on that box, you're in big trouble," she warned. "There will be no gummy turtles for you ever again."

"You'll be good, won't you, Teeny?" I said, patting him on the head.

I'd even given him a bath, and he was clean as a whistle. He smelled like bubblegum.

When we walked into the church, a heavy perfume scent stopped me dead in my tracks. There were so many flowers that the church smelled like a flower shop.

Miguel's family sat on one side, and Lyndsey's family sat on the other. That didn't make sense to me at all.

"Why can't we sit wherever we want?" I asked Mom. "This seems weird. Very weird."

"Yeah, how can Lyndsey's and Miguel's families get to know one another if they have to sit in different places?" Katie asked.

"This is just part of a wedding tradition," Nana explained. "Lyndsey's and Miguel's families will have lots of time to meet one another."

"I won't have wedding rules when I get married," said Katie.

"Don't worry, Katie," I giggled. "No one will marry you anyway!"

"Now who's trying to be funny?" said the Snoop. "Let's have a truce. No more mean comebacks. Deal?"

"Okay, okay. I *guess*," I promised my sister.

"Well, it's about time you two act like loving sisters," said Nana. "What a treat it is to see you be nice to each other. One of these days you'll be glad you have a sister. Trust me on that."

I didn't see that day happening anytime soon, but I had to believe my grandmother. Nana always told the truth.

The piano music began playing, and a few of Lyndsey's friends walked to the front of the church. Each girl held a pretty red flower with a yellow ribbon.

Miguel looked a little nervous, like he might faint. But then Lyndsey walked in, and Miguel's face broke into the biggest grin. Lyndsey looked amazing. Her dress was covered with white lace and pearls, and she even had white flowers in her hair like a princess.

And then there was the ceremony, which I thought was a little bit of a snooze fest. After what seemed like forever, the minister finally said, "I now pronounce you husband and wife."

Finally! Cake, here I come!

Miguel gave Lyndsey a mushy kiss, and Nana and Mom cried like big babies.

When we got to the reception, I marched right up to the huge three-tiered sugar bomb of a cake.

"I'd like a piece with a big rose on top," I told the lady serving the cake. "And vanilla ice cream, please."

The lady even cut two pieces for Teeny. He looked so cute in his little black bow tie.

After a while, Lyndsey and Miguel wandered around to all of the tables, thanking their guests for coming. Then they stopped at ours.

"Welcome to our family, Miguel!" said Dad. "It was a beautiful wedding."

"*Gracias*, Dr. O'Banning. Thank you so much! You must visit us again. Channing, maybe there will be a new dinosaur exhibit at the museum next time. There might even be a mesosaurus. Those dinosaurs—"

"Used to swim in water!" I said. "I know about them too!"

"Very good, Channing O'Banning," Miguel said. "You're a regular dinosaur expert!"

Miguel motioned for me to come closer, like he had a secret for me. "The lady from the turquoise mine is one of our wedding guests. We heard you paid her a visit yesterday, and I think she's looking for you."

Miguel pointed to the table where she was sitting.

Yes! How lucky am I to have cousins who know so many people?

"Be right back, Mom!" I promised and took off like a flash toward the back of the room.

"Well, there you are," said the lady from the mine. "What a coincidence that we both know Miguel and Lyndsey. I was afraid you'd forgotten." She reached into her purse and handed me a small velvet box. "I hope you like it. I think it turned out beautifully."

"Gracias, gracias!" I said, accepting the box and shaking her hand.

It was finished! I slowly raised the lid and peeked inside. The turquoise stone was polished and shiny, and the ring even had a silver leaf on the side. It looked almost like the one that I'd lost.

My cousin Lyndsey wasn't the only one getting a beautiful ring today.

I could hardly wait to find Nana.

15

Lost and Found

"Oh, Nana, I have a little something for you!" I said. "Now, close your eyes and hold out your hands."

I could hardly wait to show her. *But what if she doesn't like it?*

"For me?" squealed Nana. "Chan, what on earth are you up to?"

I placed the box in her tiny hands, and she untied the bow slowly.

"Oh my! It's beautiful! It's absolutely beautiful!" Nana gasped and slid it onto her finger. It fit just right.

"That's to replace the one that I lost at school," I reminded her.

"That is so nice of you, Channing. But you didn't have to do that. I forgave you for losing it. And guess what? I have a surprise for you too!"

Nana reached into a small bag and handed me a new pencil I decided to call Adobe Orange. But something special was also tied around the pencil: a silver and turquoise ring! It looked just like Nana's, only smaller.

"Wow!" I said. "It's awesome! Now we match! And I don't have this color of pencil either. I'll use it on my poster for Mr. Reese's class. I'll take extra-good care of both of these things, Nana."

"Good minds think alike," said my grandmother. "I'm glad that my little artist likes them both. Now that Lyndsey and Miguel are happily married, let's get ready to make one last stop in New Mexico. You'll want to draw the Taos Pueblo in your sketch-book for sure."

I stuck my new pencil into the top of my ponytail and slid my new ring onto my finger.

The ride to Taos was incredible. Now I understood what Boring Doring was trying to teach us about landforms. The rock canyons near Taos were brown, orange, purple, and yellow. Sagebrush and yellow flowers were growing everywhere too. But when we came around one curve, my mouth dropped wide open.

"Oh my!" Mom said, pointing through the windshield. "There's the Rio Grande Gorge. It's like the earth just opened up!"

"You can say that again," said Katie. "That thing is massive!"

"And do you know what caused that big crack in the earth?" I asked confidently. "Erosion. And that's the Rio Grande River flowing through. It goes for miles and miles."

"Wow," said my sister, giving me the strangest look ever. "You know more about rocks than I thought. You sorta sound like Cooper—you know— *like a brainiac.*"

I guess I paid more attention in Boring Doring's class than I realized.

"Being a brainiac is cool if you ask me," Nana said proudly. "Even Teeny agrees. After all, he's a genius pig." Nana always knew what to say to make me feel better.

Dad pulled off to the side of the road, and we took tons of pictures of the Rio Grande Gorge. We looked so tiny compared to the ginormous landform behind us.

After traveling a few more miles, we finally made it to Taos and parked in front of the largest pueblo I'd seen yet.

This had to be it.

"We don't have much time, but we can't go back to Greenville until we've seen this very special place," said Dad.

"I studied about the Taos Pueblo in school, but I didn't think I'd ever see it for real," I said. "There's even a picture of this in my social studies book."

"Well, then, would you like to tell us all about it?" asked Mom. "I'm sure Mr. Reese would be very proud."

I went on to explain that the Pueblo people had lived here for more than one thousand years and had been attacked by the Spanish long ago. There was no electricity in the pueblo, and their water came from a little stream out front called Red Willow Creek.

The closer I looked at the Taos Pueblo on the left side of the stream, I noticed there was also another large pueblo on the right. Strangely, even though both buildings were three stories tall, I didn't see any stairs—only lots of small windows and bright blue doors. *Weird, very weird.*

"How do they get up there?" I asked, pointing to the upstairs doors. "Mr. Reese didn't teach us about that."

Luckily Dad had purchased a brochure at the front gate. "Apparently they use those tall wooden ladders over there. In earlier days, they would climb up an outside ladder to the roof, and then use another inside ladder to go down a small hole into their homes. If there was a Spanish attack, they could quickly pull in the outside ladders and no one could get in. How would you like to climb a ladder to get to your bedroom at home?" he asked.

"I wouldn't mind!" I said. "That sounds super fun!"

"It also says here that most of the people speak their native language, called Tiwa, as well as English and Spanish," Dad said, surprised.

"Wow, I have trouble knowing just one language!" said Katie. "Maybe I'll try harder studying Spanish in school."

"Yeah, me too," I agreed. "Or I guess I should say *sí*."

"Count me and Teeny in on that as well," said Nana. "That crazy pig will never understand the difference between 'gracias' and 'thank you,' but you know Teeny—he hates being left out!"

Before we headed to the airport, we enjoyed some delicious treats at the pueblo: roasted corn on the cob and warm fry bread. Special spices were sprinkled on the buttery corn, and the fry bread tasted like a big fluffy tortilla.

Teeny went bonkers over the corn. I mean *really bonkers*. He snorted, smacked, and zipped through that corn, cob and all.

"Look at him go!" Nana said. "That crazy pig has gone cuckoo over corn!"

"Think you could make corn that tastes like this when we get home?" I asked Nana. "This is the best stuff ever!"

"It sure melts in your mouth," she said. "But I doubt it. It just gives us another reason to make a return visit to Taos!"

"I agree with Nana," said Katie. "This place is awesome."

If only Maddy and Cooper could have been there with me to see the Taos Pueblo. But since I knew they'd never forgive me for the dinosaur disaster, they certainly wouldn't believe that I'd seen this world-famous building. Just thinking about Cooper and Maddy made me sad all over again. I wished I could stay in New Mexico.

There has to be a pueblo for embarrassed artists somewhere.

During the plane ride home, I made a list of everything I wanted to include in my Native American assignment. After everything I'd seen, I hoped I'd have enough room for it all! I never would have guessed that my art poster would include pottery, jewelry, woven rugs, and adobe pueblos. But now it all made perfect sense. Anyone who created something with his or her own two hands was really an artist. Even if it was a wedding blanket or a silver and turquoise ring, each one was a work of art and could be shared with someone special.

Come to think of it, Nana's baking is a form of art. She picks out her ingredients, creates something unique (like my favorite cookies), and likes watching others enjoy them. There's more to art than just a sketchbook and colored pencils. And the more I think about it, the more I realize that God is the most incredible Artist of all. He created this beautiful planet full of colorful places, and we get to enjoy looking at all of them. I sure hope I can see even more cool places with my family—and with Teeny of course.

As soon as we got home, I raced to my room, got out my art materials, and asked Mom to help me print photos from the trip. This assignment was going to be a breeze.

But I super dreaded going to school the next day. I didn't even touch my pancake topped with gummy turtles the next morning.

"Chan, I know you don't want to see Maddy and Cooper. But I bet they've already forgotten all about the . . . well, you know . . . the dinosaur mix-up."

"I hope you're right, Mom. My stomach is kind of queasy. Maybe I'll wait and go to school tomorrow."

"You'll feel better once you get to school," Mom said. "Now scoot, or you're going to be late."

As soon as I got there, the first two people I saw were Maddy and Cooper at the lockers.

Yikes.

"Uh, hi, Maddy," I said quietly, looking down at my sneakers.

"Hey, Chan! Where did you go on winter break? I tried calling you a dozen times," Maddy said.

"Huh? You *did*?" I asked.

"So did I," said Cooper. "Did you vanish or what?"

"You two really wanted to talk to me?" I asked. "I didn't think you'd ever speak to me again, after the, well, you know."

"Oh, *that*?" said Cooper. "Maddy and I weren't mad at you, Channing."

"You weren't?" I asked happily.

"No—I mean it was embarrassing that we

thought concrete was a dinosaur," Maddy said, "but we'd all been digging thinking it was going to be something awesome. That wasn't your fault. And after all, it *was* kind of fun digging around in those rocks and stuff. Even if it was just a piece of concrete."

"And we have a surprise for you!" said Cooper.

Whew! It was such a relief to have my best friends back. Mom and Nana were right all along. Suddenly, Cooper reached into his pocket and held out his hand. I could hardly believe my eyes.

It was Nana's ring.

"You found it! You found it!" I screamed. "Where was it?"

"At the dig site," said Cooper. "I guess something good came out of that hole after all."

It must have fallen off my finger the morning I looked for Maddy and Cooper at school.

Now Nana would have two rings!

"Coop, you're the best!" I said, giving him a high five. Not only did my friends forgive me, but they even found Nana's treasured ring in that crazy concrete mess.

"Chan, are you ever going to tell us where you've been?" Maddy asked as we walked to class.

"I went to my cousin's wedding in New Mexico,"

I said. "Mr. Reese was right—the Wild West is a cool place. You won't *believe* the tons of dinosaurs they have out there!"

Maddy and Cooper looked at each other and smiled. I knew exactly what they were thinking . . .

But this time I took a picture!

The End

Did You Know?

1. There are approximately two million Native Americans in the United States and one million in Canada. There are more than two hundred tribes, which can be as different from one another as the Chinese culture is from American culture. If you want to learn about Native American culture, the best idea is to pick a specific Native American tribe to study. Then, if you are very interested, you can learn about a second tribe and compare one tribe to another. All are very different and fascinating! (www.native-languages.org/kidfaq.htm)

2. The Taos Pueblo in New Mexico is the largest multi-storied pueblo in the United States and is considered a national landmark and World

Heritage Site. Check out www.indianpueblo.org /19pueblos/taos.html for more interesting information.

3. All Native Americans hunted and eventually domesticated animals. Most tribes used as much of the animal as they could. Meat was used for food. Furs and skins were used for clothing and shelters. The stomach was used to carry and hold water. Bones were used for needles and weapons.

4. The most important Native American food crop was corn, or what they called maize. Other important American Indian crops included squash, potatoes, wild rice, tomatoes, sweet potatoes, beans, pumpkins, and peanuts. Native American tribes also had diets that included meat such as elk, buffalo, rabbit, deer, salmon, turkey, goose, pheasant, and shellfish.

5. Early Native Americans had different types of shelter, depending on where they lived. Some lived in tepees, some in log homes called hogans, and some even in homes made out of blocks of ice.

6. The Native American tribes began to diminish when white settlers moved onto their lands. The Spanish, for example, attacked many

Pueblo tribes. Many Native Americans were eventually moved onto lands called *reservations*. Many died from disease during these forced moves. These were very sad times for Native American people.

7. November is Native American History Month. Use this special time to learn more about their culture so that you can appreciate them all year around!

Check out the following websites for more information!

www.native-languages.org

www.kidskonnect.com

Want to read more about Channing O'Banning? Check out www.channingobanning.com and find out where the famous fourth grade artist is going next!